Usborne Forgotten Fairy Tales

The Nettle Princess

Retold by Rob Lloyd Jones

Illustrated by Alessandra Santelli

Reading consultant: Alison Kelly

About
Forgotten Fairy Tales

People have been telling
each other fairy tales for
thousands of years. Then,
a few hundred years ago,
collectors began writing the
stories down. The ones that
became famous were the
ones that reflected the ideas
of the time.

These stories had patient, polite princesses such as *Snow White* and *Sleeping Beauty*. The tales with bold girls fighting their own battles were ignored.

This series brings to life the stories of those forgotten brave and brilliant girls…

Contents

Chapter 1

Secret meetings

There was once a princess called Elisa, who loved a prince called Hans. Hans loved Elisa too, so much that he felt his heart might burst.

Elisa's father was at war with Hans's father. So Hans and Elisa met in secret, in a forest between their kingdoms.

Elisa loved the forest almost as much as she loved Hans. She even loved the stinging nettles.

"You are the only person who talks to nettles," Hans joked. But that was one of the reasons he loved her.

Elisa's father, the king, grew suspicious. "I have decided that you will marry a duke from our kingdom," he announced.

Elisa refused to let her father rule her life.

I certainly will not!

The king's face turned red with rage. He rose from his throne and roared to a guard. "Take her to the Tower!"

Chapter 2

The Tower

Guards marched Elisa to
a stone tower on a hill. They
threw her inside with sacks of
oats and barrels of water.

"You will stay in there for five years," the king barked. "So you learn to obey me."

The guards sealed the entrance, leaving Elisa alone in the dark.

Elisa was determined to escape. She scrambled to the wall, and began to scratch at the stones with her nails.

Months passed. Still Elisa kept scratching.

A little ray of sunlight shone through a hole in the wall. Still she kept scratching.

As she worked, she spoke
to a little nettle growing on
the ground. She told it about
Hans and the forest.

13

A whole year passed. More rays of sunlight shone into Elisa's gloomy prison.

Finally, one of the stones began to wobble. "It's loose!" Elisa gasped.

Chapter 3

Escape!

Elisa leaned against the wall and pushed the loose stone. She felt very weak, but she thought of seeing Hans, and pushed harder.

At last the stone fell away.
Elisa tumbled through the gap
in the wall...

Oof!

...and landed with a thump on
the grass outside.

She jumped up, squinting
in the brilliant daylight.
"Hey, she's escaped!"
a guard cried.

Elisa fled. The
guard chased her
across her father's
kingdom to
the forest.

Exhausted, Elisa hid
among a patch of nettles.
The guard came closer...

Finally, the guard turned
and trudged away.

The nettles hadn't stung Elisa at all. "Thank you my friends," she said. "You saved me."

Elisa set off for Hans's kingdom. Would he still love her, after all this time?

Chapter 4

Maid Elisa

Elisa's heart pounded as she reached Hans's palace. She feared she would be sent straight home to her father.

At the gates, her path was blocked by a grim-faced guard. "You must be Lady Olga's new maid," the guard grunted. "Follow me!"

The guard led Elisa to Lady Olga's room. "About time!" Lady Olga cried.

"What wedding?" Elisa asked.

Lady Olga's lips curled into a sneer. "*My* wedding, of course. To Prince Hans."

Chapter 5

Wedding plans

That night, Elisa watched
the moon rise over the forest.
"I am a fool," she breathed.
"Of course Hans forgot me."

She decided to run back to the forest, to live alone among the trees. But the next morning, she was stopped again by Lady Olga's guard.

The guard led Elisa to Lady Olga's bathroom door. The lock had broken, and Lady Olga was trapped inside.

"My wedding is about to start," Lady Olga screamed. "Everyone is waiting for me!"

"My maid must go instead,"
Lady Olga insisted. "If she
wears a veil, Hans will never
know it's not me."

Before Elisa could refuse,
servants had dressed her for
the ceremony.

A guard marched Elisa
to the palace chapel. She was
about to flee, when the
wedding guests parted and
she saw...

"Hans!" she gasped.

Chapter 6

Wedding day

Elisa stared at Hans from across the chapel. He looked the same as when they were last together in the forest.

He took her arm and they walked to the altar. Suddenly, Elisa stopped. "Wait!"

The prince had been about to step on a nettle. Elisa guided him away, and then crouched to the plant.

"Little friend," she whispered, "you are safe now."

Elisa didn't notice Hans staring at her, his mouth open in astonishment.

As the wedding began, Hans kept gazing at Elisa. She looked away, scared he would realize she was not his true bride.

By the time the ceremony finished, Lady Olga was free. "Give me back my dress," she demanded.

Lady Olga rushed to join Hans at the wedding feast. When she lifted back her veil, Hans looked even more confused.

As Elisa watched, she saw
Hans whisper to his new
bride. The last pieces of
her heart crushed to
dust, and she fled.

But Elisa had not heard
what Hans had whispered
to Lady Olga...

"Did you talk to that nettle?" he had asked.

"What?" Lady Olga had replied. "Why would I talk to a silly *nettle*?"

Now, Hans was sure that something very strange had happened...

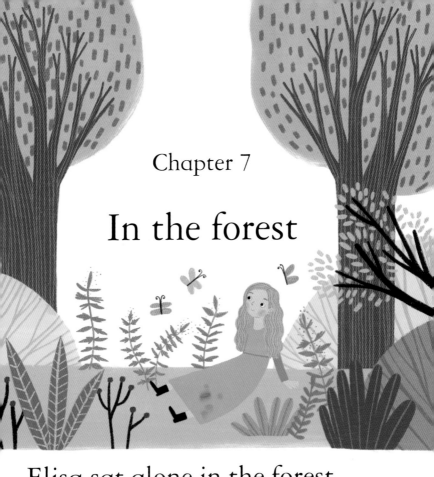

Chapter 7

In the forest

Elisa sat alone in the forest.
She watched butterflies
flutter, sunlight fall through
branches, and nettles swaying
in the soft breeze.

"Oh, nettles," she sighed,
"I have nowhere left to go.
But at least I still have you."
    "I only know one person
who talks to nettles,"
a voice replied.

Elisa whirled around. She
hid behind the nettles, as
Hans appeared.

"Elisa," Hans said, "I do not need to see you to know it is you. But... I was told you were dead."

"*Dead?*" Elisa burst from hiding, filled with sudden fury. "Who told you that lie?"

"My father," Hans explained. His cheeks turned red with shame. "He forced me to marry Lady Olga. Unlike you, I was not strong enough to refuse. Will you forgive me, now that we are married?"

"Married?" Elisa didn't understand. "Hans, you married Lady Olga."

Hans sank to one knee and took Elisa's hands. The nettles stopped swaying, and all the creatures in the forest stopped to watch.

"No," Hans said.
"I married the person
who stood beside
me at the altar.
That was you."

Elisa forgave Hans. They lived together in the forest, where they built a small home.

Every day, they walked
among the trees. Elisa always
said hello to her friends,
the nettles.

About the story

The story behind *The Nettle Princess* was first written down in 1845, by German language expert Karl Müllenhoff, although no one's quite sure where he first heard the tale.

Later, brothers
Wilhelm and Jacob
Grimm added it to their
collection of fairy tales,
calling it 'Maid Maleen'.

Designed by Laura Bridges
Series designer: Russell Punter
Series editor: Lesley Sims

First published in 2020 by Usborne Publishing Ltd.,
Usborne House, 83-85 Saffron Hill, London EC1N 8RT, England.
usborne.com